The Maskless Ra

Written and Illustrated by
Danielle Rueger

Not too far from here a small neighborhood stood
with houses and lawns right beside a small wood.

Deep down in that wood there was quite a hubbub
as two raccoon parents welcomed their new cub.

He was almost perfect: ten fingers, ten toes,
dark rings on his tail and a cute button nose.

But something was missing from his little face...

Their cub had no mask! None at all! Not a trace!

"My goodness!" said Mother. "Oh what should we do?"
The father raccoon shrugged, then realized he knew.

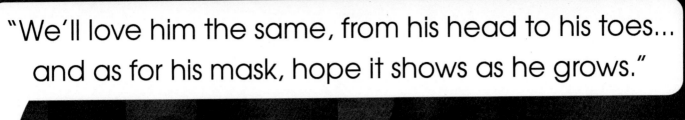

"We'll love him the same, from his head to his toes... and as for his mask, hope it shows as he grows."

They looked at their baby with nothing but love and chose the name Phillip for their little cub.

Well, Phillip got older, but still had no mask.
To other raccoons he was quite the outcast.

Then one night as the group was on its way out
young Phillip called all of them back with a shout.

"Hey guys! Just this once, do you think I could go?"

The group looked at Phillip and quickly said "no".

"We're sorry to say it, but just have to ask,
Why would we invite a raccoon with no mask?"

Well, Phillip was hurt with no clue what to say.
He choked back a tear and he went on his way.

With nowhere to turn Phillip trudged down a street...

Until he was scared by a loud...,

"Trick or Treat!"

Young Phillip saw humans in masks at a door
They all asked for treats then went next door for more.

The costumes were cool. Phillip wanted to stay,
but humans nearby means raccoons go away.

"If humans make masks," Phillip thought, "why can't I?"
That moment help started to fall from the sky.

Raindrops hit the ground landing with a soft thud,
until all the dirt Phillip stood on was mud.

He dipped his tail in, then applied mud with grace.
Carefully, he formed a neat mask on his face.

He looked in a puddle to see how he'd done.
He added some more. Might as well make it fun.

He loved it all:
getting to
scavange and play,

and being with other
raccoons every day.

Until one night
they were out messing around...

From nowhere large raindrops began to pour down.

He ran from the rain and tried to cover up...

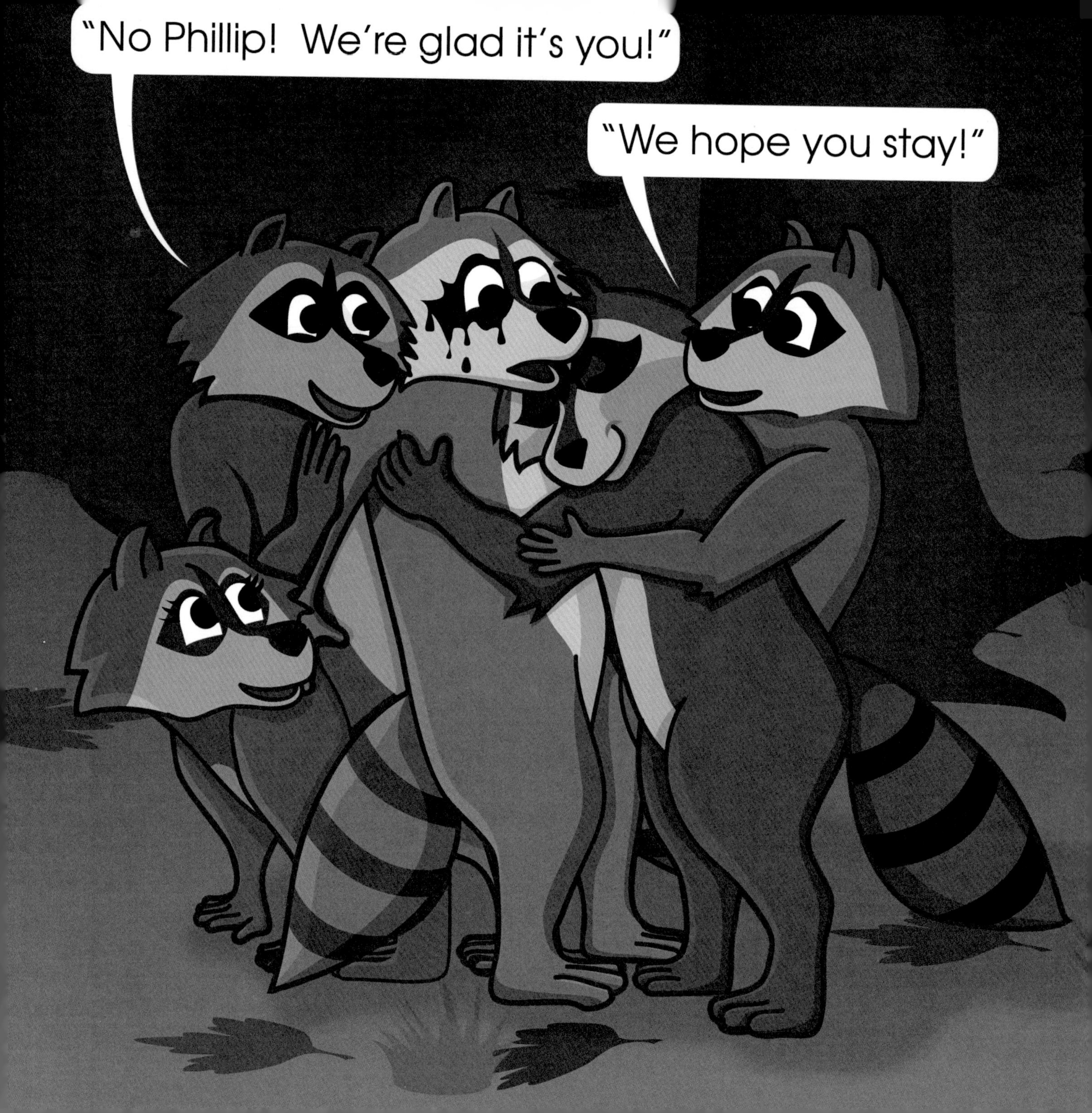
"No Phillip! We're glad it's you!"
"We hope you stay!"

"That's easy!" said Phillip. "Some mud's all this took."

"That's awesome!"

"Think you could give me a new look?"

Which led to how Phillip spent his time that day:
Creating masks, each unique in their own way.

Now Phillip was glad his mask never appeared
He had found his talent because he was "weird".

Phillip was the happiest he'd ever been.
By being himself, he finally fit in.

Not Buddy, but Phillip, the maskless raccoon
and this thought put Phillip right over the moon.